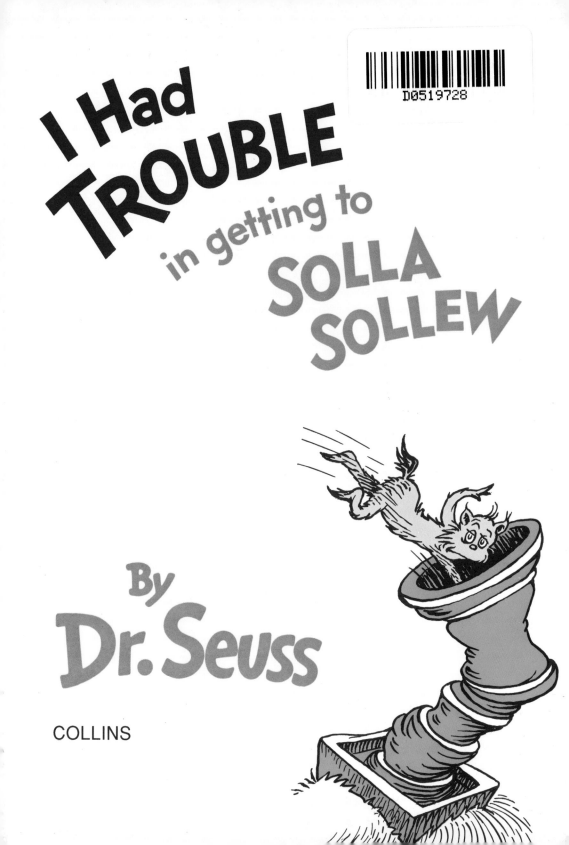

I Had TROUBLE

in getting to SOLLA SOLLEW

By Dr. Seuss

COLLINS

D0519728

The Cat in the Hat
™ & © Dr. Seuss Enterprises, L.P. 1957
All Rights Reserved

CONDITIONS OF SALE
The paperback edition of this book is sold subject to the
condition that it shall not, by way of trade or otherwise,
be lent, re-sold, hired out or otherwise circulated
without the publisher's written consent in any form of
binding or cover other than that in which it is published
and without a similar condition, including this condition
being imposed on the subsequent purchaser.

6 8 10 9 7

ISBN 0 00 171614 X

© 1965, 1993 by Dr. Seuss Enterprises, L.P.
All Rights Reserved
Published by arrangement with Random House Inc.,
New York, USA
First published in the UK 1967
First published in this edition 1998 by
HarperCollins*Children's Books,*
a division of HarperCollins*Publishers* Ltd

Printed and bound in Hong Kong

for
Margaretha Dahmen Owens
with love
and with thanks

I was once happy and carefree and young
And I lived in a place called the Valley of Vung
And nothing, not anything ever went wrong
Until . . . well, one day I was walking along
And I guess I got careless. I guess I got gawking
At daisies and not looking where I was walking. . . .

And that's how it started.
Sock! What a shock!
I stubbed my big toe
On a very hard rock
And I flew through the air
And I went for a sail
And I sprained the main bone
In the tip of my tail!

Now, I never had ever had
Troubles before.
So I said to myself,
"I don't want any more.

"If I watch out for rocks
With my eyes straight ahead,
I'll keep out of trouble
Forever," I said.

But, watching ahead . . .
Well, it just didn't work.
I was watching those rocks. Then I felt a hard jerk.
A very fresh green-headed Quilligan Quail
Sneaked up from the *back* and went after my tail!

And I learned there are troubles
Of more than one kind.
Some come from ahead
And some come from behind.

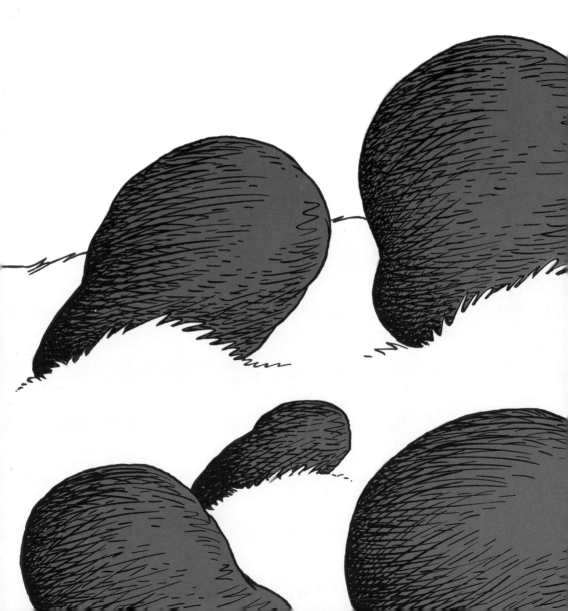

So I said to myself, "Now, I'll just have to start
To be twice as careful and be twice as smart.
I'll watch out for trouble in front and back sections
By aiming my eyeballs in different directions."

I found this to be
Quite a difficult stunt.
But now I was safe
Both behind and in front.

Then NEW troubles came!
From *above!*
And *below!*
A Skritz at my neck!
And a Skrink at my toe!
And now I was *really* in trouble, you know.
The rocks! And the Quail!
And the Skritz! And the Skrink!
I had *so* many troubles, I just couldn't think!

There I was,
All completely surrounded by trouble,
When a chap rumbled up in a One-Wheeler Wubble.
"Young fellow," he said, "what has happened to you
Has happened to me and to other folks, too.
So I'll tell you what I have decided to do. . . .
I'm off to the City of Solla Sollew
On the banks of the beautiful River Wah-Hoo,
Where they *never* have troubles! At least, very few.

"It is not very far.
And my camel is strong.
He'll get us there fast.
So hop on! Come along!"

I jumped up behind him. Then all through that day
The Wubble wubbed on in a wubble-some way.
The road got more bumpy, more rocky, more tricky.
By midnight, I tell you, my stomach felt icky.
And so I said, "Mister, please, when do we get
To that wonderful town? Aren't we almost there yet?"
"Young fellow," he told me, "don't get in a stew.
At sunrise, we'll drive into Solla Sollew
And you'll have no more troubles. I promise. I do."

But, when dawn finally came and the darkness got light,
That wonderful city was nowhere in sight.
Instead of the city, we ran into trouble.
Our camel was sick and he started to bubble.
We had to pull *him* in the One-Wheeler Wubble!
So there, there we were in a dreadful position.
Our camel now needed a camel physician.

Now, doctors for camels are not often seen.
Especially on mountains. They're far, far between.
But we pulled that old Wubble and set out to find
Some doctor, while dragging our camel behind.

I pulled, pulled and pulled. Then the next thing I knew,
I was pulling the camel *and Wubble chap, too!*
"Now, really!" I thought, "this is rather unfair!"
But he said, "Don't you fuss. I am doing my share.

"This is called teamwork. I furnish the brains.
You furnish the muscles, the aches and the pains.
I'll pick the best roads, tell you just where to go
And we'll find a good doctor more quickly, you know."
Then he sat and he worked with his brain and his tongue
And he bossed me around just because I was young.
He told me go left. Then he told me go right.
And that's what he told me all day and all night.

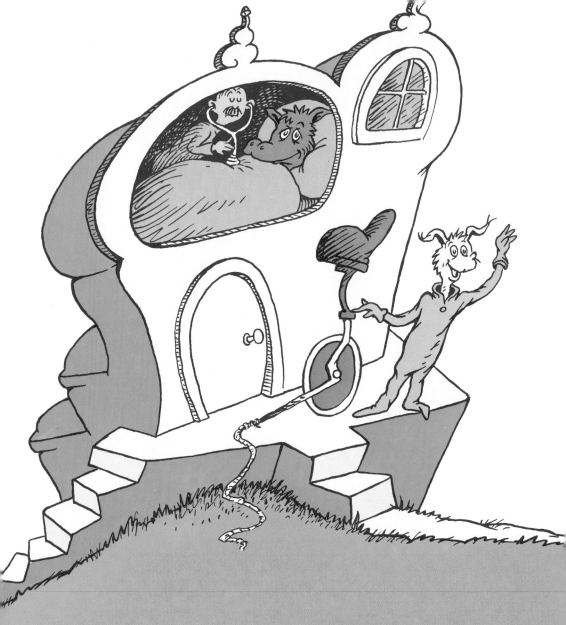

Next morning we located Dr. Sam Snell,
Who knew all about tonsils and camels as well.
Our camel, he said, had a bad case of gleeks
And should lie flat in bed for at least twenty weeks.

I was tired. How I wanted to crawl in that bed!
But the Wubble chap sent me away and he said,
"Your troubles are practically all at an end.
Just run down that hill and around the next bend
And you'll come to the Happy Way Bus Route, my friend.
The Happy Way Bus leaves at 4:42
And will take you directly to Solla Sollew
On the banks of the beautiful River Wah-Hoo,
Where they never have troubles. At least, very few."

Well . . .

The bus stop was there. And that part was just fine.

But tacked on a stick was a very small sign

Saying, *"Notice to Passengers Using our Line:*

We are sorry to say that our driver, Butch Meyers,

Ran over four nails and has punctured all tyres.

So, until further notice, the 4:42

Cannot possibly take you to Solla Sollew. . . .

"But I wish you a most pleasant journey by feet.
Signed
Bus Line President, Horace P. Sweet."
So I went on by feet, thanks to Horace P. Sweet.
And that Horace P. Sweet almost ruined my feet!

A hundred miles later
My feet were so sore!
THEN, wouldn't you know it!
It started to pour!

I was drenched to the skin when a chap in a slicker
Splashed up and he yelled, "It's the Midwinter Jicker!
The Midwinter Jicker came early this year
And it's not going to be very comfy 'round here.
Any fool would get out! So I've packed up my things
And I'm off to my granddaddy's, out in Palm Springs.
Take cover!" he yelled. "Use my house if you wish."
Then the chap in the slicker splashed off like a fish.

I ran in the house and I fell in a heap.

I needed my rest, but I just couldn't sleep.

Did *you* ever sleep, when your feet were like ice,

With a family of owls and a family of mice?

I listened all night to the growls and the yowls

And the chattering teeth of those mice and those owls,

While the Midwinter Jicker howled horrible howls.

I tossed and I flipped and I flopped and I flepped.

It was quarter past five when I finally slept.

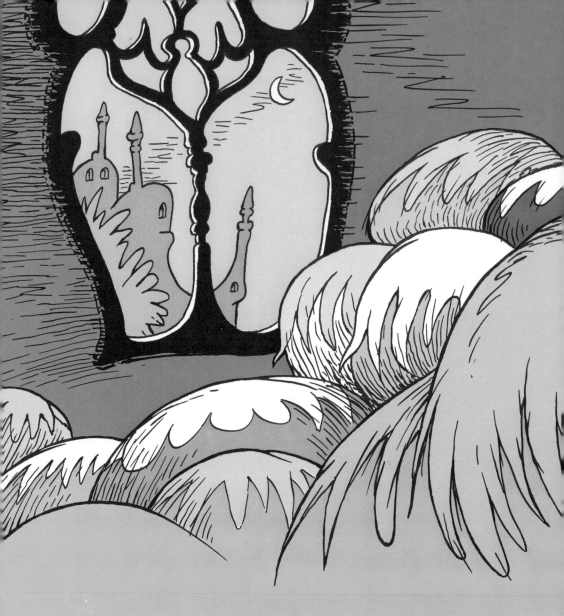

Then I dreamed I was sleeping on billowy billows
Of soft silk and satin marshmallow-stuffed pillows.
I dreamed I was sleeping in Solla Sollew
On the banks of the beautiful River Wah-Hoo,
Where they never have troubles. At least, very few.

Then I woke up
And it just wasn't true.
I was crashing downhill in a flubbulous flood
With suds in my eyes and my mouth full of mud
And my nose full of water, my ears full of shrieks
Of the owls flying off with the mice on their beaks!
And I said to myself, "Now I really don't see
Why troubles like this have to happen to *me!*"

I floated twelve days without toothpaste or soap.
I practically, almost had given up hope
When someone up high shouted, "Here! Catch the rope!"
Then I knew that my troubles had come to an end
And I climbed up the rope, calling, "Thank you, my friend!"

I got to the top. But it *wasn't* a friend!

And I saw that my troubles were *not* at an end.

A big man on a horse scared me out of my wits.

He bellowed, "I'm General Genghis Kahn Schmitz.

"There's a war going on! And it's time that you knew
Every lad in this land has his duty to do.
We're marching to battle. We need you, my boy.
We're about to attack. We're about to destroy
The Perilous Poozer of Pompelmoose Pass!
So, get into line! You're a Private, First Class!"

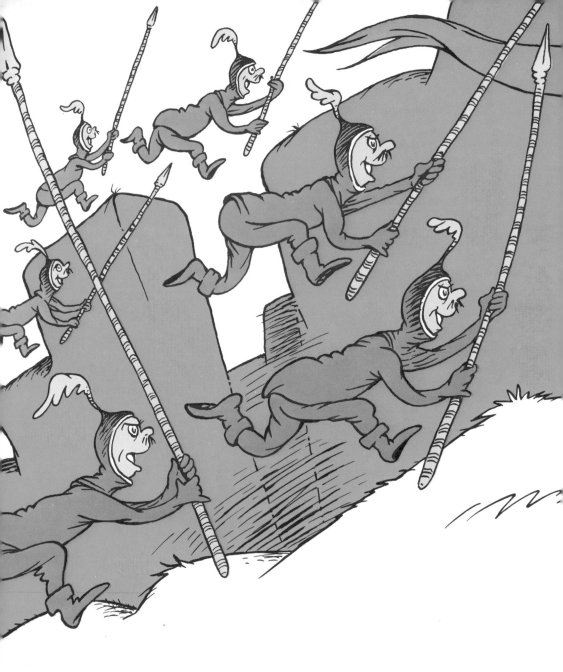

He gave me a shooter
And one little bean,
Which was not very much,
If you see what I mean.

Then he yelled, "Get that Poozer! Attack without fear!
The glorious moment of victory is near!"
And the glorious general led the advance
With a glorious swish of his sword and his lance
And a glorious clank of his tin-plated pants.

Then we went 'round a corner and found that, alas,
There was *more* than one Poozer in Pompelmoose Pass!
And Genghis Kahn Schmitz shouted out to his men.
"This happens in war every now and again.
Some times you are winners. Some times you are loosers.
We *never* can win against so many Poozers
And so I suggest that it's time to retreat!"
And the army raced off on its tin-plated feet.

There I was!
With more Poozers than I'd ever seen!
There I was!
With my shooter and only one bean!
There I was!
And I thought, "Will I ever get through
To the wonderful city of Solla Sollew
On the banks of the beautiful River Wah-Hoo,
Where they never have troubles, at least very few?"

I had terrible trouble in staying alive.
Then I saw an old pipe that said, "Vent Number Five."
I didn't have time to find out what *that* meant,
But the vent had a hole. And the hole's where I went.

Well . . . that vent where I went
Was a sort of a funnel
That led me down into
A frightful black tunnel.
The traffic down there
Was a mess, I must say,
With billions of birds
Going all the wrong way.
They bumped me with bikes
And they banged me with dishes.
I ran into ladders,
Beds, bottles and fishes.
I skidded on rubbish.
I fell in a horn.
Troubles! I wished
I had never been born!

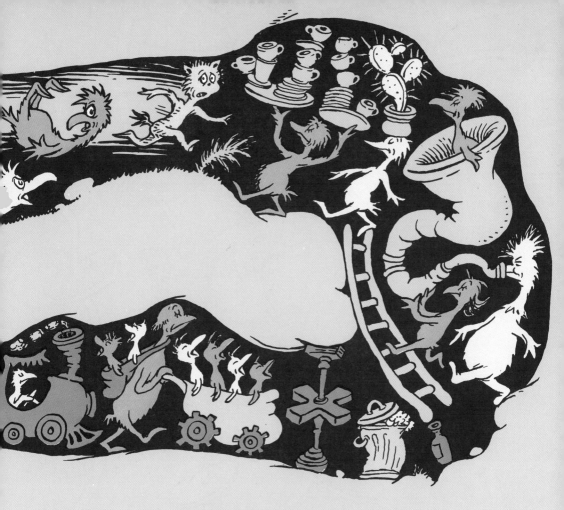

I was down there three days in that bird-filled-up place.
At least eight thousand times, I fell smack on my face.
I injured three fingers, both thumbs and both lips,
My shinbone, my backbone, my wishbone and hips!
What's more, I was starved. I had nothing to eat.
And damp! Was it damp! I grew moss on my feet!

VOTE
FOR
SFINDEX

Then, just when I thought I could stand it no more,
By chance I discovered a tiny trap door!
I popped my head out. The great sky was sky-blue
And I knew, from the flowers, I'd finally come through
To the banks of the beautiful River Wah-Hoo!
I couldn't be far, now, from Solla Sollew!

There it was! With its glittering towers in the air!
I'd made it! I'd done it! At last I was there!
And I knew that I'd left all my troubles behind
When a chap at a doorway that shimmered and shined
Waved me a wave that was friendly and kind.

"Welcome!" he said as he gave me his hand.
"Welcome, my son, to this beautiful land.
Welcome to sweet, sunny Solla Sollew,
Where we never have troubles.
At least very few.
As a matter of fact, we have only just one.
Imagine! Just one little trouble, my son.
And this one little trouble,
As you will now see,
Is this one little trouble I have with this key. . . .

"There is only one door into Solla Sollew
And we have a Key-Slapping Slippard. We do!
This troublesome Slippard moved into my door
Two weeks ago Tuesday at quarter to four.
Since then, I can't open this door any more!
And I can't kill the Slippard. It's very bad luck
To kill any Slippard, and that's why we're stuck
And why no one gets in and the town's gone to pot.
It's a terrible state of affairs, is it not!

"And so," said the Doorman of Solla Sollew,
"My job at the door here is finished. I'm through!
And I'll tell you what I have decided to do. . . .

"I'm leaving," he said, "leaving Solla Sollew
On the banks of the beautiful River Wah-Hoo,
Where we never have troubles, at least very few.
And I'm off to the city of Boola Boo Ball
On the banks of the beautiful River Woo-Wall,
Where they never have troubles! *No troubles at all!*
Come on along with me," he said as he ran,
"And you'll never have *any* more troubles, young man!"

I'd have no more troubles . . .
That's what the man said.

So I started to go.
But I didn't.
Instead . . .
I did some quick thinking
Inside of my head.

Then I started back home
To the Valley of Vung.
I know I'll have troubles.
I'll, maybe, get stung.
I'll always have troubles.
I'll, maybe, get bit
By that Green-Headed Quail
On the place where I sit.

But I've bought a big bat.
I'm all ready, you see.
Now my troubles are going
To have troubles with *me!*